MEET THE CONES

By Chris Madeley
Illustrated by Zara Hussain

Fisher King Publishing

Meet The Cones
Copyright © Chris Madeley 2014
ISBN 978-1-910406-05-2

Illustrated by Zara Hussain

Published by
Fisher King Publishing
The Studio
Arthington Lane
Pool-in-Wharfedale
LS21 1JZ
England

For my dearest Grandchildren
who all believe:
Marielle, George, Max,
Henry, Rachel and Ben.
Keep Cone-spotting!

Many companies and organisations
have been wonderfully supportive
during the creation of the Cones series
of books including:

Q Parks Ltd

HA Fox Jaguar Leeds

NSPCC

Enjoy Digital

Down a long street in the big city there stands a very tall building.

On the top floor, in a special office, works a Very Important Person.

He sits behind a huge desk with piles of paper on either side of him.

The Very Important Person looks worried and scratches his head.

"What am I going to do?" he asked himself. "All my motorways and roads are getting worn out and really need mending.

"This is going to be very dangerous for the cars, buses and trucks and it will be dangerous for the road workers, too.

"The Police are far too busy to help me, so how am I going to make it safe for everyone?"

"...what I need is something to help move the traffic safely..."

"...a bright warning sign that everyone will take notice of."

The Very Important Person thought hard and his face went bright red! He leaned back in his big chair, thinking and thinking and thinking...

Suddenly, he jumped to his feet, threw his hands in the air and shouted "Yes! Yes! **Yes!**" in a very loud voice.

There was a timid knock on the office door and a scared-looking face peeped inside.

"Come on in!" Said the Very Important Person to his Assistant.

"Are you OK?" she asked.

"Oh yes!" he laughed. "I have just worked out how to direct the traffic safely as we mend the roads."

"IMPOSSIBLE!" she said. "The only safe way is to make everyone stay at home, and you can't do that!"

"I don't want people to stay at home," said the Very Important Person.

"I want people to go to work and go out to have lots of fun. My roads are for driving on and they should not be closed for mending! What we need are CONES!"

"Cones? How can little biscuity things help you control the traffic?" Asked the Assistant.

"Not ice cream cones, silly! Big, bright red Cones all standing together in rows!" Said the Very Important Person.

The road workers and Police were delighted to hear the Very Important Person's plans and all he had to do now was to have the Cones made – but even he had no idea what was about to happen next.

The Cone Factory was very busy and everyone was rushing around to make sure the Cones were finished before home-time. Night was falling and in the darkening sky the stars awoke and twinkled merrily.

The workers heard the welcome sound of the factory hooter telling them that their day's work was done. Row after row of shiny new Cones were left standing neatly in the factory.

The sky outside was as black as velvet and the stars gleamed like millions of tiny light bulbs in the frosty air. Up came the beautiful New Moon, shiny and bright, high into the night sky.

This was a very special night. It was one of those rare nights when ancient magic from the beginning of time stirs and begins to work its enchanted spell. There was a strange feeling in the air, as if the whole world was holding its breath and pausing to see what would happen next.

When the moon is new
and just on the right tilt,
When the air is cold and the
stars shine brightly,
As the clock strikes midnight
and there is no breeze,
Moondust falls down the curve
of the moon and streams
Twinkling down to earth,
and where it lands
Wonderful things happen.

This night was one of those nights. Look, can you see how the Moondust falls through the darkness?

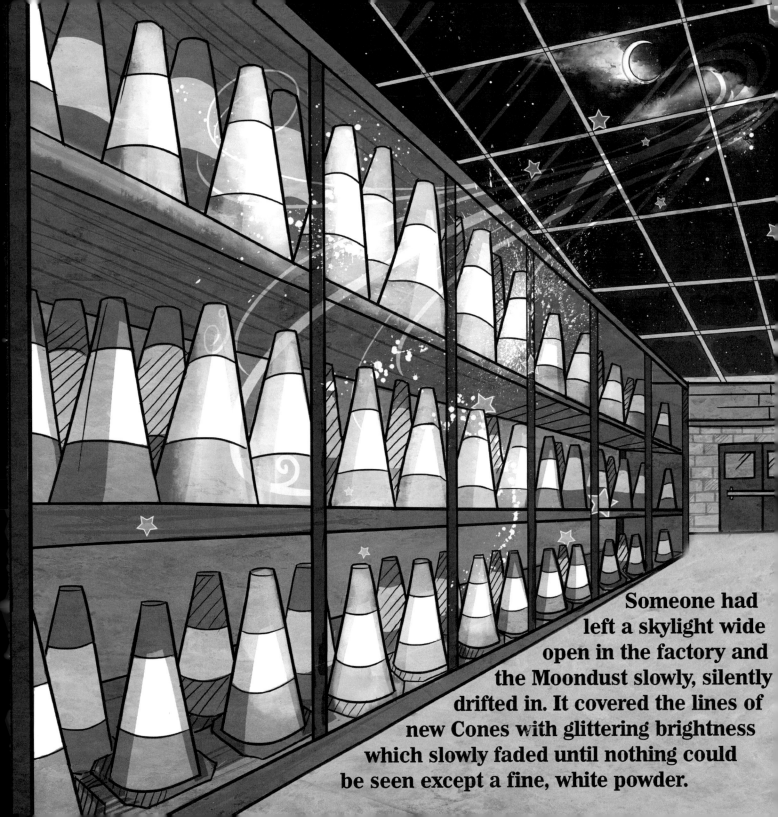

Someone had left a skylight wide open in the factory and the Moondust slowly, silently drifted in. It covered the lines of new Cones with glittering brightness which slowly faded until nothing could be seen except a fine, white powder.

"Aaahh!" One of the Cones let out a deep sigh and stretched its arms.

"Oh!" Another Cone looked surprised and blinked. "What's all this?"

"Well, that's just great!" said the first Cone pointing his finger at the other Cones. "All bright, shiny and new and then someone drops dust all over us. Grrrrrr!"

The other Cones joined in, stretching and shaking to remove the dust and brushing it off each other with their hands. Soon the whole factory was buzzing with chattering Cones.

"Why are we here?"

"What are we doing?"

"Where are we going?"

"What do we do?"

The Cones were amazed that they could speak to each other and the noise grew louder and louder as they became more and more excited.

Suddenly, a door opened with a loud crack. A bright torch snapped on and in walked the Night Security Guard. He thought he had heard a noise and wanted to make sure everything was safe. He would be in serious trouble if anything happened to the Very Important Person's precious Cones.

At that very instant a most peculiar thing happened. Faster than the blink of an eye, the Cones became Just Cones. No faces, no voices, no hands, no movement: Just Cones. This is the first Cone Rule. When a human eye looks at the Cones, they become Just Cones.

Early the next morning dozens of trucks drove into the factory yard and parked in a straight line.

The factory workers hurried through the gates to see what was happening.

Back in his office, the Very Important Person was combing his hair and straightening his tie. He was very excited because today was the day that his brilliant idea was going to be put into action.

"Someone will need to be in charge of the Cones," he said to his Assistant, "and as it was my idea I think it should be me. Now what should I call myself? Erm, Cone. . . Cone. . . what is the word? I know, I will be the Conetroller!"

The Conetroller drove down to the factory in his big black car and turned slowly into the factory yard.

The factory workers were waiting outside and there was silence as the Conetroller walked proudly across the yard and climbed onto a small platform so that everyone could see him.

The Conetroller cleared his throat to speak. "Ladies and gentlemen," he said in a very loud voice, "thank you all very much for making my Cones. Now everyone will be safe as my roads are mended. Hurry now, load the Cones onto the trucks. Away you go, but do remember, drive safely!"

The trucks were soon loaded and everyone cheered as they drove out of the yard to begin their journey to the roadworks up and down the country.

Later that day the biggest truck carrying the most Cones slowed down as he came to a very long motorway. The Cones were dropped in a neat, straight line, so that the traffic could be directed away from the roadworks.

When the last two Cones were put down, the truck roared away into the distance, leaving behind hundreds of new Cones, their reflective safety stripes shining brightly in the soft evening light.

For a few minutes nothing happened. The Cones stood exactly where they had been put down. Then, the Cone at the end opened one eye and closed it again quickly.

A few seconds later he opened one eye again and then opened the other one. Slowly he looked around.

Next to him all the other Cones were standing neatly in a line as far as the eye could see.

He decided to speak to the Cone standing next to him. This Cone, like all the others, was being Just a Cone, no face, no voice, no hands, no movement. Just a Cone.

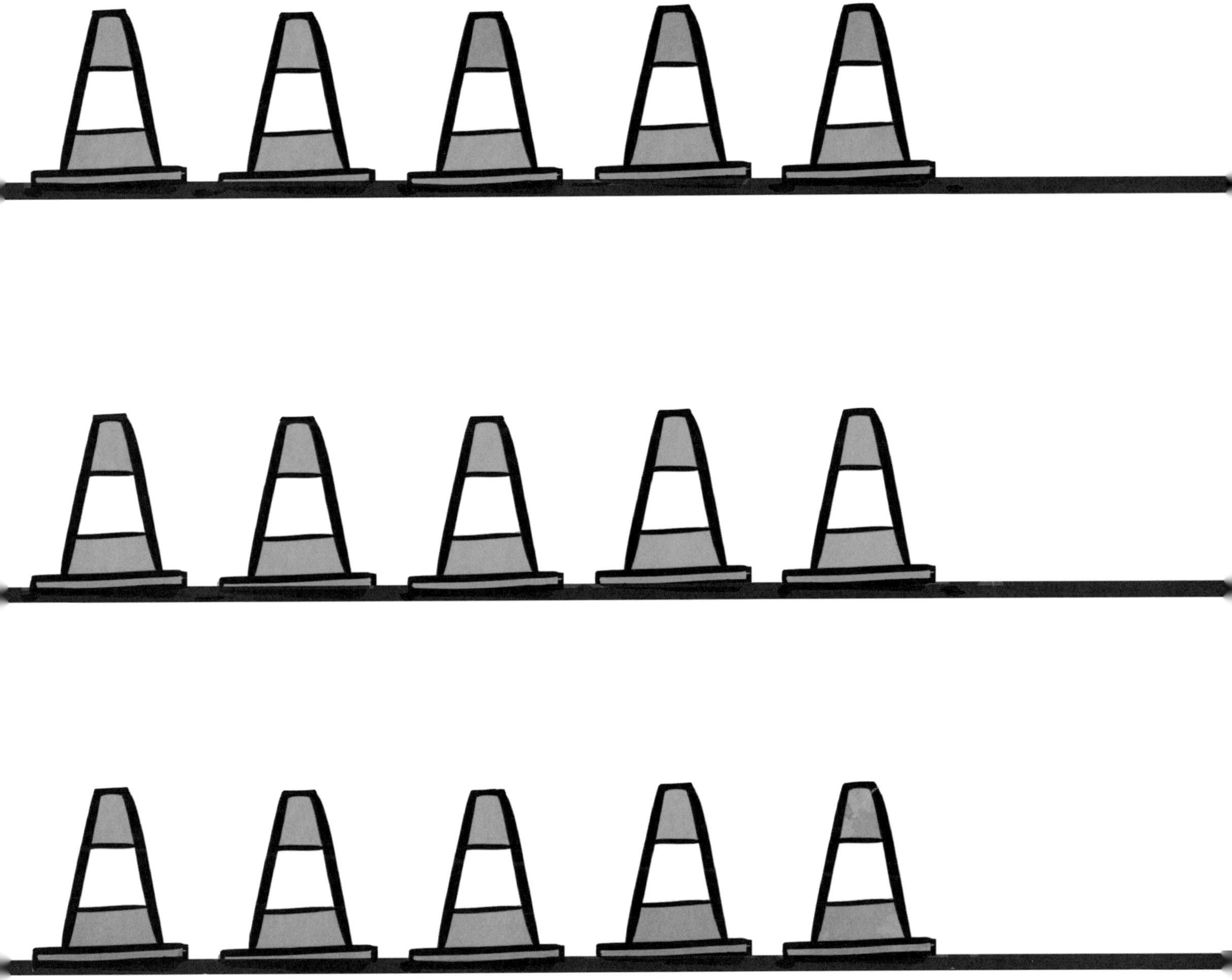

"Hello Cone! Are you there? This is **BRILLIANT!**"

The Cone next to him spoke. "What do you mean?"

"Well, the Conetroller said we have to keep everyone safe. Look at the cars, trucks and buses. They are on *that* side of our line so that the workers on *this* side are kept safe as they mend the roads.

"And there is something else. I've been thinking about a name for myself because it is going to get very 'conefusing' if we call each other 'Cone,' isn't it? Anyway, I have decided to call myself Conerad. I think you are a very pretty Cone. What are you going to call yourself?"

She thought for a moment then it came in a flash, "I shall be called... Conestance." She said with a satisfied smile.

"I like your name, Conestance. I hated being stacked on that truck. I couldn't see or move. Trucks are smelly, bumpy things and they bang us together which makes me feel sick!" said Conerad in a disgusted voice.

"Oh, I agree! I am going to be a very good Cone and then I shall never have to be stacked on a truck ever again," said Conestance thoughtfully.

"Look, the workers are going home and the sun is setting. I think it is time to go to sleep now. Night night, Conestance. See you in the morning."

So, the two new friends became Just Cones.
No faces, no voices, no hands, no movements.
Just Cones.

At that moment, Police Car drove steadily up the motorway and parked on his look-out point above the Cones. "Good night, Cones," he purred softly, "sleep tight. You have a lot of work to do."

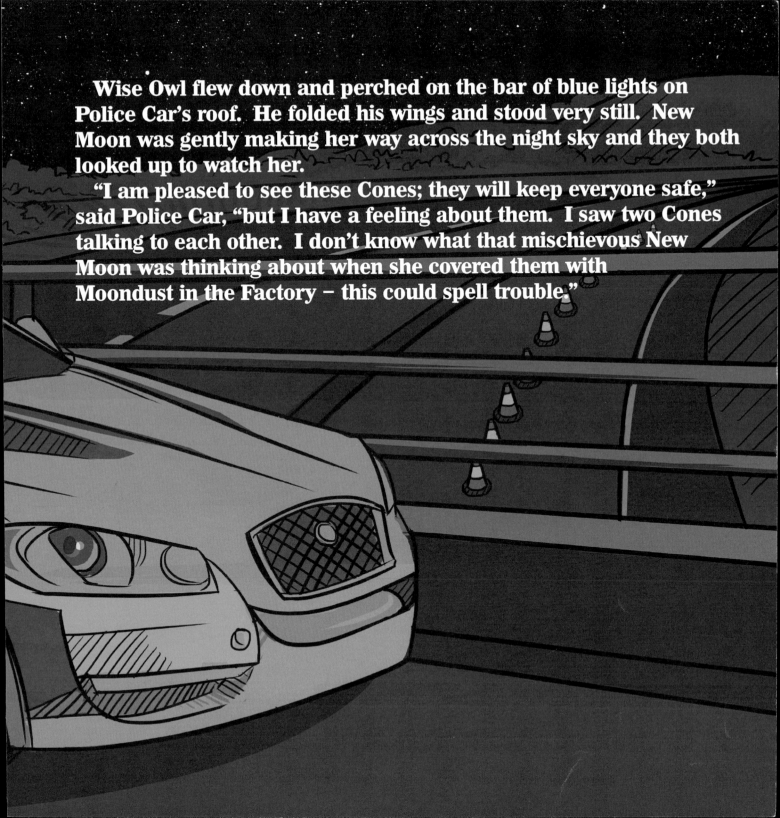

Wise Owl flew down and perched on the bar of blue lights on Police Car's roof. He folded his wings and stood very still. New Moon was gently making her way across the night sky and they both looked up to watch her.

"I am pleased to see these Cones; they will keep everyone safe," said Police Car, "but I have a feeling about them. I saw two Cones talking to each other. I don't know what that mischievous New Moon was thinking about when she covered them with Moondust in the Factory — this could spell trouble."

"Whooooo hooooo. I agree with yooooo hooooo," hooted Wise Owl.
Police Car frowned. "It will be our job to keep an eye on them.

"I expect they could get into
lots of trouble and
up to all sorts of
mischief if we are
not careful."

"Toowhoooo
Troowhooo.
Toowhoooo Troowhooo,"
hooted Wise Owl and he
spread his beautiful wings,
stretched up onto his tiptoes
and flew off into the dark
night.

So, Children, our Cones are
now in place, but do you
remember the Moondust?...

...Who knows what will happen next? Join me again soon
for more adventures with the Cones.
Goodbye for now.

Lightning Source UK Ltd.
Milton Keynes UK
UKRC02n0122171117
312758UK00003B/65